≈≈≈≈≈≈≈

When she was younger, Renee never dreamed of having a husband as successful as James. But a savings account couldn't keep her warm at night. She rarely complained about his work hours, but today she looked forward to her man being there when she got home.

"My day keeps getting worse," she griped.

"Baby, it's not that bad. You'll still be up when I get home."

"Maybe I will. Maybe I won't."

"I'll make it worth your while," James promised.

Renee smiled. She was certainly eager for him to try. But they had a hurdle in the sex department, and she doubted if James was willing to jump it tonight. *How long has it been?* she wondered. She figured at least three months had passed since the last time she was able to coax him into it. Renee decided she was due, if not because of the time that passed, then at least for the terrible day she'd been having.

"Are you gonna hurt me?" she asked tentatively. Her heart was already starting to race.

After a noticeable pause, James said, "No. But I will make love to you, as a husband should make love to his wife."

That was his typical response. Renee was not deterred.

"What if I don't want you to make love to me?"

"I don't know," he said. "I guess you can go to sleep horny."

Renee found this banter amusing, but she didn't want him to know that.

"I'm having a terrible day," she reiterated. "And it's been a long time since you did that for me."

"It hasn't been that long," James said. "It was Saturday, April 13th."

Renee was stunned by that. "You remember the exact date?"

"When a man does those things to his wife, it's not easy to forget."

"You make it sound like it's hurting you in some way."

"Renee, I'm working just as hard as you are today. I don't want any trouble when I get home."

"You're probably gonna have some."

"I'm not going there with you tonight. I'm serious."

"I understand that you're serious. I want you to be serious."

"Stop playing around."

"Only if you make me."

He sighed loudly into the phone. "I love you, baby. But you're starting to piss me off."

"Perfect," she said. "That's a good start."

"Renee, it's not gonna wor–"

She hung up on him.

≈≈≈≈≈≈≈

HARDER

HARDER

An erotic novella

KEITH THOMAS WALKER

KEITHWALKERBOOKS, INC
This is a UMS production

HARDER

KEITHWALKERBOOKS

Publishing Company
KeithWalkerBooks, Inc.
P.O. Box 331585
Fort Worth, TX 76163

For information write
KeithWalkerBooks, Inc.
P.O. Box 331585
Fort Worth, TX 76163

All characters in this book have no existence outside the imagination of the author and have no relation whatsoever to anyone bearing the same name or names. They are not even distantly inspired by any individual known or unknown to the author and all incidents are pure invention.

This book is intended for Adult Audiences Only. It features sexual encounters, graphic language and situational violence that may be considered offensive. Please keep away from minors.

ISBN-13 DIGIT: 978-0-9882180-1-7
ISBN-10 DIGIT: 0988218011
Library of Congress Control Number: 2013912947
Manufactured in the United States of America

First Edition

Visit us at www.keithwalkerbooks.com

*This book is for anyone who has ever
wanted it HARDER*

*Big thanks to my readers who stick with me as
I experiment with different genres. Know that
even with erotica, the story is always most
important to me.*

MORE BOOKS BY
KEITH THOMAS WALKER

Fixin' Tyrone
How to Kill Your Husband
A Good Dude
Riding the Corporate Ladder
The Finley Sisters' Oath of Romance
Blow by Blow
Jewell and the Dapper Dan
Harlot
Plan C (And More KWB Shorts)
Dripping Chocolate
The Realest Ever
Jackson Memorial

Novellas

Might Be Bi Part One

Visit keithwalkerbooks.com for information
about these and upcoming titles from
KeithWalkerBooks

ACKNOWLEGMENTS

Of course I would like to thank God, first and foremost, for giving me the creativity and drive to pursue my dreams and the understanding that I am nothing without Him. I would like to thank my wife for being my first and most important critic, and I would like to thank my mother for always pushing me to be the best I can be. I would like to thank Janae Hafford-Hampton for being the best advisor, supporter and little sister a brother could ever have. I would also like to thank (in no particular order) Brandy Rees, Denise Bolds, Sabrina Scott, Dianne Guinn, Kierra Pease, Sharon Blount, BRAB Book Club, Trey Williams and Uncle Steven Thomas, one love. I'd like to thank everyone who purchased and enjoyed one of my books. Everything I do has always been to please you. I know there are folks who mean the world to me that I'm failing to mention. I apologize ahead of time. Rest assured, I'm grateful for everything you've done for me!

CHAPTER ONE
A BAD START

If buttons could talk, Renee's would've said, "*Are you serious? Stop that! I can't... Wait a minute, I'm trying to – I said hold on! I can't, I'm just... Alright, I'm outta here!*" a moment before jerking to the left at a suicide angle and then being forcibly ripped from the only home it had ever known in her denim jeans.

It didn't pop off completely, but it wobbled like a lose tooth, and there was a small hole in her favorite jeans where the button was once firmly attached. Renee was lying on her back on her un-made bed. She was attempting to squeeze her size fourteen hips into a pair of size twelve jeans when the tragedy occurred. Renee sighed, and her stomach expanded, quickly relishing the freedom from the confined space she tried to force it into. From her vantage point, she couldn't see past her belly roll, but she fingered the loose button and knew exactly what had happened.

"Ain't this some bull," she muttered aloud in the quiet room.

Renee hopped off the bed and checked herself in the full-length mirror next to her dresser. Despite this new reminder that she hadn't started the diet she'd been saying she would start for the past six weeks, she couldn't help but smile at her predicament. Her jeans flared into bell-bottoms around the ankles, but from the knees up, they looked like they could've been painted on. Renee turned slightly and saw that her ass was as plump as ever. The blouse she planned on wearing with the outfit revealed quite a bit of her dark chocolate cleavage.

If she had managed to get her jeans buttoned, Renee would've been busting out all over the place – which was probably not what her employer had in mind for *casual Friday*. Renee thought about a poster she'd seen on the internet. It featured a scandalously-clad black woman who looked totally out of place in a crowded office filled with cubicles. The caption read, "LaKeisha ruins casual Friday for everyone!"

"Yeah, bitch, that's you," Renee told her reflection. She laughed, unaware that this morning's fashion mishap was just the beginning of a stress-filled day.

A peek at her alarm clock revealed that it was 7:45 am. She had to leave no later than eight to have time to pick up two coworkers who were carpooling with her and make it to the office by nine.

Renee peeled the jeans down her thighs (which were too thick according to the charts in her doctor's office – but Renee never got any complaints from her man), and she nearly fell when she tried to step on the cuffs and shake the denim off her feet. She raced to the closet and quickly determined that none of her other jeans would work with the blouse she picked out for the day. She had a beautiful pair of Capris that would be perfect, but they were in the laundry bin.

Much to her dismay, Renee had to scrap her outfit completely in favor of a tan dress with floral prints. It looked nice on her, but she could wear a dress any old day. Casual Friday meant she could wear comfortable sneakers to work, but the dress required a pair of pumps or heels.

Renee raced through her home for the next fifteen minutes finding it hard to believe how one, little button could change so much. She had to make sure her legs had a coat of cocoa butter lotion because of the dress, and then she struggled with her choice of footwear because until she got a pedicure, open-toed sandals were not an option. Thankfully her hair didn't get messed up during the wardrobe change, but her coffee got cold, as did the breakfast burrito she planned to eat before she left the house.

Renee didn't have time to reheat either, because at eight o'clock she realized she couldn't find her keys. She left them on the dining room table yesterday – in the same spot she always left them. Her immediate suspicion was that one of the kids had bothered them. But today was July 5th, and the boys were spending the month with their father. Renee dashed through her house frantically, eventually looking in places she would *never* leave her keys, like the bedroom dresser and even the refrigerator.

At 8:05 she grabbed her cellphone and started to call her husband, but one last search of the dining room proved fruitful. Her keys were on the table, exactly where they should be, mostly concealed by a large bag of gummy bears. By then Renee wanted very badly to have someone to blame her morning troubles on, but she knew that she purchased the candy when she stopped to get gas on the way home from work yesterday. When she came in, she placed her keys and the candy in the same spot and hadn't thought about it again until this moment.

"Fuck!" she growled as she snatched up her keys. She took the candy, too, because she really didn't give a damn about a diet, and she was fairly certain gummy bears were as much a part of a nutritional breakfast as Cheerios were. She didn't need the FDA to second that. Her grumbling stomach told her it was so.

Renee wanted to run back to the bathroom to check on the perspiration that accumulated on her face while she rushed about her home like a mad woman, but the last thing she needed was to show up late for work *again*. Plus she didn't have on any make-up, other than lipstick, so she could fix her face when she got in the car.

≈≈≈≈≈≈≈

Thirty minutes later Renee was going 35 mph on E. Berry with two passengers in her Honda Civic. Despite the hectic start, they were set to arrive at the Houston Tower on 6th Avenue a few minutes before their shift started at nine o'clock. All three ladies were employed by Work Ready staffing office, where they took calls from businesses as far away as Dallas. Their job was to help companies with their temporary staffing needs by utilizing a huge list of employees who had a variety of qualifications. The work wasn't very rewarding, but the pay wasn't bad, especially considering there was no college degree required for their position.

Lynda sat up front with her iPad displaying the only page Renee had ever seen it on; a game called FarmVille. Michelle sat up straight in the backseat, busying herself with what looked like a full course meal. She had one of those fancy paper plates with built-in partitions. One section had two sausage patties, another had scrambled eggs, and the largest had a Belgian waffle smothered in syrup and butter. Renee would've questioned how the girl managed to eat such a meal in a moving vehicle, but she'd seen it plenty of times before. Even when it was Michelle's turn to do the driving, she still managed to eat a hearty breakfast.

Today Renee was super envious – not only because Michelle could pig out every day and yet maintain her petite physique, but also because the aromas from her coworker's meal were absolutely delectable and were starting to make her mouth water.

"Girl, if you don't hurry up and finish that plate," she called to the backseat, "I'm gonna have to pull over, so you can split it with me."

"Oh, I'm sorry," Michelle said. She looked up and met Renee's eyes in the rearview mirror. "I can give you some. I didn't know you were hungry."

Like Renee, Michelle was in her early thirties. She had straight, black hair and the fullest set of lips Renee had ever seen on an Asian woman.

"I'm just kidding," she said.

"No, she ain't," Lynda said without looking up from her game. "I been listening to your stomach growl for the past ten minutes. You know you're hungry," she said to the driver.

Renee laughed good-naturedly. Out of all of the women at the office, Lynda had always been her favorite. She was old enough to be her mother and had a lot of motherly wisdom. Renee never would've gotten involved with carpooling if Lynda hadn't talked her into it.

"I am hungry," Renee admitted.

"I see you gobbling them gummy bears," Lynda said. "I guess today won't be the day you start your diet then..."

If that had come from a different co-worker, Renee would've been defensive. But after working together for the past six months, she was accustomed to Lynda's habit of telling-it-like-it-is. Lynda once told her, "The only thing that needs sugar-coating is food. People don't have time to figure out what the hell you're trying to tell them." That was in response to Renee attempting to be polite while informing Lynda that her makeup looked atrocious one day. Since then, the ladies had become good friends.

"I think I'm going to wait 'til school starts in August," Renee said. She was about as convincing as her high school prom date swearing he just wanted to put the *tip* in. That failed experiment left Renee with a chubby baby boy named Paul.

"I know I said I wanted to get right for the summertime," Renee said. "But the summer's almost over anyway..."

Lynda looked up at her and grinned, but she didn't respond.

"I was going to start my diet this weekend," Renee went on, reading her mind. "I was thinking, with the boys away with their daddy, I won't have to cook as much. But me and James went to a pool party on Saturday, and he said I looked *very nice* in my two-piece." Renee smiled, thinking of the way he openly admired her body. Renee knew that her husband adored her hips and ass. The fact that he didn't mind her pudgy tummy made her feel even better.

"If you're happy, and James is happy, that's all that matters," Lynda said. "You know you look just fine to me. I know a lot of people who need to go on a diet – me being the first one – but your figure is perfect for you."

Michelle continued eating quietly in the back seat. She learned a long time ago that when women were discussing their weight problems, the last thing they wanted was an opinion from someone who maintained a size four with no effort.

"I broke a button on my jeans this morning," Renee confided.

Lynda looked up at her and tried her best to stifle a snicker.

"They were my favorite jeans," Renee said. "I had my whole outfit planned."

Lynda couldn't help but laugh then. "I can just imagine you trying to squeeze your hips into some too-little jeans! It wasn't enough when you had to hold your breath to get them on. You had to keep trying until you lost a button!"

Michelle laughed too, but she caught herself and tried to keep a straight face.

"It's okay to laugh," Renee said. She giggled as she watched her in the rearview mirror. "I wouldn't have told y'all, if I didn't think it was funny."

"And after that, you made a decision *not* to start your diet..." Lynda said.

"I think those pants shrunk in the wash," Renee explained.

"Yeah, and those gummy bears didn't have nothing to do with it!"

Renee laughed merrily. The laughter didn't distract her from the road, but she did wipe her eyes a split second before a pint-sized terrier decided to dart across the street.

"*Oh hell! Watch out!*" Lynda yelled, but Renee had already begun reacting to the hazard.

Her right foot moved to hit the brakes, and her hands jerked the steering wheel hard to the right to avoid plowing down the pooch. Unfortunately her hands moved faster than her foot. Renee barely had a chance to muster a scream before her vehicle veered dangerously towards the curb, and her whole life flashed before her eyes.

"*Hold on!*" she bellowed, a split second before her front wheel encountered unyielding concrete with a bone-rattling impact that felt like they got rear-ended. The Honda was by no means an off-road vehicle, but Renee rolled six-feet through someone's well-manicured lawn before she pulled the wheel to the left, finally bringing her car to a stop on the street again.

Her hands gripped the steering wheel so tightly her fingers were numb. Renee stared straight ahead, her breaths coming quick and hot. Both of her passengers were screaming, but they quieted down after a few moments. Renee put her car in PARK but was afraid to take her foot off the brake. Her heart hammered as she looked around and asked, "Is everyone okay?"

"What happened?" Michelle screeched. Her thin eyes were widened to nearly comical proportions.

"Damn dog ran in front of me!" Renee shouted. As the initial shock dissipated, she was glad her car's seatbelt held true and equally grateful that the airbags did not deploy. She looked over at Lynda who had not spoken and was taking shallow breaths with a hand resting daintily over her chest. Renee's jaw dropped.

"Oh my God! Lynda! Are you okay?"

The older woman nodded. She took a few more slow breaths with her eyes locked on the street ahead of them. Renee was horrified, thinking her friend was having a heart attack. But Lynda shook her head slowly and finally looked in her friend's direction.

"Just scared me, that's all." A smile softened her features. "I'm too old to be getting in car accidents."

"*I'm sorry!*" Renee said. She was exasperated.

"It wasn't your fault," Lynda said. "Nothing you could do."

"I should've ran that little bastard over!" Renee exclaimed. She turned to check on her other passenger. "You okay?"

"I'm fine," Michelle said, and Renee saw that her safety belt kept her secure as well. "Wow. Felt like a roller coaster!"

Michelle smiled, which relieved a lot of Renee's tension, and she grinned too. That was until she saw that the contents of Michelle's breakfast plate were strewn around the backseat like vomit. Sticky syrup was everywhere – everywhere except on Michelle for some reason. She was the only thing back there that remained unblemished.

"Oops. Sorry. I dropped my plate."

Renee couldn't blame her for that, but she had to ask, "How come none of it fell on *you*?"

"I don't know," Michelle said, looking around. "Don't be a hater."

Renee burst into laughter. Michelle rarely spoke in slang, and she always sounded out of place when she did.

≈≈≈≈≈≈≈

There was no laughing, however, when they got out to inspect the damage. Renee's two second off-road excursion left a trail of damaged grass in some poor sap's lawn. But more importantly, the tire on the passenger's side of Renee's car was completely deflated.

Closer inspection revealed a dent in the rim itself. The three ladies stared at the problem in silence before Lynda shook her head and said, "Your husband's gonna kill you."

Renee knew that wasn't the case. James was a smart and thoughtful man. He'd be concerned for her safety, but anger was an emotion he rarely showed.

"You have a spare?" Michelle asked.

"Yes. But I don't know how to change it. Do you?"

Michelle shook her head. "You have to take the hubcap off first."

"There is no hubcap," Renee said. "It's over there." She pointed to a spot in the lawn she'd partly mangled. They all saw the plastic hubcap glinting in the morning sun.

"See, I don't even know what they look like," Michelle said. "All I know is, you have to take the hubcap off first."

"Can you call your husband?" Lynda asked.

Renee shook her head. "I can, but it won't do any good. He had to go to work at four this morning. He can't answer his phone when he's at work."

"Aww, lookey," Michelle said.

Renee followed her gaze to a cute, little fur ball that had come to investigate the wreck.

"*That's* the bastard that ran me off the road!" Renee shouted and pointed.

The terrier recoiled from her but didn't run away.

"He's so cute," Michelle cooed. She approached the minuscule menace and knelt so that she could pet him. "He's scared to death," she gushed. "*Aww, him so precious.* He has a tag. Maybe we can find his owner. Wait, it's a *girl!*"

Renee didn't give a damn about that mutt – unless maybe she could sue the owner for letting it terrorize the roadways like this.

"My husband's at work, too," Lynda said. "But I can call one of my sons. I hope the axle isn't bent." She stared at the damaged wheel woefully.

"No, I'll call Triple A," Renee said. "They'll probably get here just as fast. And they can help me get it towed, if there's something else wrong with it."

The axle? Jeez. She hoped it was just the flat tire. James might cop an attitude after all if it turned out she risked their lives *and* caused serious damage to her vehicle while trying to save some wayward terrier. She frowned at the dog and fished her cell phone from her purse.

"I'll call work," Lynda offered. "I hope Betty's not too upset about us being late today."

Ugh! Renee's whole demeanor changed at the thought of their crabby supervisor.

Lynda saw her expression and said, "It's not your fault that we had an accident. It should be okay."

For anyone else, it might have been. But Renee had already exhausted her verbal warnings for tardiness at work. And she was fairly certain their overbearing supervisor was out to get her.

"If you tell her I hit a curb, and there was no one else involved, it will be my fault," Renee guessed.

Lynda waved her off as she made her phone call. Renee returned to her car to get Triple A's number from her insurance information.

CHAPTER TWO
GETTING WORSE

After getting the tire changed, they arrived at work over an hour late.

"So, it was just you involved? No other vehicle?"

Broom Hilda, better known as Betty, the supervisor, stared down her wart-covered nose at her capricious employee, just as Renee knew she would. Well, Betty's nose didn't have a lot of warts – not even one, to be exact. And she didn't really look like a witch. She was tall and beautiful, to be honest. She had honey-colored skin and long hair with auburn highlights. But she was evil, that much was certain. Renee saw that she took pride in belittling her for today's tardiness.

"It was still an accident," Renee said. "A lot of people have accidents with no other car involved."

Betty's office was small and stuffy. Renee hated it there, and it showed in her discomfort. The supervisor didn't even offer a nice chair for the minions she summoned to berate. Betty's executive chair had plush cushions covered with new leather. The chair across from her desk was hard and wooden. Renee had only been in the office for a couple of minutes, and her ass was already starting to hurt.

"Not a lot of people," Betty said smugly. "I'm glad everyone arrived safely, but the fact of the matter is you were late – *again*. And this time you caused two coworkers to be late as well."

Renee's mouth fell open, and it snapped closed just as quickly. Did this heifer not understand the word *accident*?

"I know it wasn't your fault," Betty said, reading her mind. "But, Renee, you've been late three times in the past 90 days. It's time to escalate things past a verbal warning."

"I never got a verbal warning," Renee interjected.

"Yes you did," Betty said. She opened a folder that had been sitting inconspicuously on her desk. "On April 23rd you arrived at eight minutes after nine. I was getting on the elevator as you were getting off, and I said, *'Renee this is your third tardy in three months. You have to tighten it up.'*" She read from her folder as she spoke. Renee wondered if she wrote the exact sentence in there.

"But you didn't say that was a verbal warning."

Betty looked up at her and smiled. "Renee. If I *verbally warn* you about being late, then that's a *verbal*-warning, isn't it?"

Renee's eyes widened. *Oh no she isn't talking down to me*! She didn't need this shit. Her husband had a great job. She only took this position because being a stay at home mom got boring. Plus it didn't hurt to have extra money in her account, for when she wanted to buy a new purse or something. Thinking of her sweet *whatever* fund, Renee managed to maintain composure.

"What I meant was, I thought you had to sit me down and sign something for an official verbal warning."

"You seem to have a lot of experience with these procedures. Is that how things worked at your last job?" Betty asked, still smiling. "I'll bet that was nice. At *this* company we only need your signature for a written warning," she said and then turned the folder around and pushed it across the desk.

Renee saw that this was indeed an official written warning, with the dates and times of her four late clock-ins printed clearly. She hated her supervisor, but she knew that she only had herself to blame. That's the problem with thinking your job is not that important. By the time you realize it is, you might have a witch like Betty breathing down your neck, just itching for you to do *one more thing* so she can send you to Human Resources to get your pink slip.

Renee decided to eat crow (with a large helping of humble pie) for the sake of her youngest son's birthday, which was coming in a few weeks.

"I'm sorry. I won't be late again," she said as she signed the damning paperwork.

"I'm sorry it had to come to this," Betty said. She watched her carefully, to make sure Renee didn't sign someone else's name, perhaps. "Hopefully there won't be any more occurrences. It's great to see you dress professionally on casual Friday, by the way. I think you might be a go-getter after all."

"Thank you." Renee hurried out of the office before some of the bad words in her head came tumbling out of her mouth.

≈ ≈ ≈ ≈ ≈ ≈ ≈

The first part of the work day seemed to fly by, probably because they were an hour late. But that didn't mean it didn't suck. Every client Renee spoke to had some sort of issue that required multiple phone calls, rescheduling and even one call that had to be escalated when the client threatened to stop using their staffing company. Renee had to transfer the foreman to Betty and then sit through another lecture afterwards about how she could've handled the client better.

By lunchtime, Renee really did want to quit. She called her husband who was home from work and about to take a midday nap.

"Must be nice," she grumbled.

"What's wrong, baby?"

"This has been a day from hell," Renee complained. She sat in the company break room frowning at a Lean Cuisine microwavable meal that was hot and ready but didn't look appetizing at all. Renee usually left the office for lunch, but her break was only 45 minutes, and she was afraid to risk returning even one minute late.

"I found your jeans on the floor," James said with a chuckle. "I guess you're going shopping this weekend."

Renee couldn't help but grin at that. A lot of men would've jumped at the opportunity to criticize her weight. But James' response to his woman getting bigger was to get her bigger clothes. That kind of love is priceless.

"I had a car accident this morning," Renee told him.

"What? When?" James' baritone voice was immediately laced with concern. "Why didn't you call me?"

"You were at work," she said. "You couldn't have done anything. You don't even have your ringer on when you're working."

"I still want to know about it. Are you alright? What happened?"

Renee told him about her run-in with the absurdly cute pooch.

"You should've hit him," James said. "No dog is worth your safety – or even damage to your car. Did the guy check everything out underneath, to make sure nothing else was damaged?"

"He didn't jack it up high enough to look at everything, but he said it was fine."

"I'll take it to the dealer tomorrow," James said. "We'll get you a new wheel. Are your friends alright? No one was hurt?"

"We're fine," Renee said. "Except Michelle spilled a whole plate of food in the back seat. There's syrup everywhere. And then I got wrote-up for being late when I got here."

"They wrote you up for having a car accident?" James was incredulous.

"My sup' doesn't like me," Renee explained. "She said this is my fourth time being late in three months."

"Oh. Well..."

"Well what?"

"Why have you been late so much? I didn't know about that."

Of course he didn't. James was up and out of the house before the crack of dawn on most days.

"I had an accident today," Renee stressed. "I shouldn't get written-up for having a car accident."

"Okay." James decided to save his lecture on responsibility for later. "You sound stressed, baby. Want me to have a bath ready for you when you get home?"

"Ooh, baby, that would be so ni–"

"Aww, shit. I don't even know why I offered. I'm not going to be here when you get home."

Renee's stomach suddenly felt sour. She felt like the only bright spot in her day just got blotted out by more rain clouds. "Don't tell me you have to work tonight."

"They fired all of those guys," James reminded. "Now they're paying overtime to cover their shifts. I think it's stupid. But hey, I'm making a killing until they get it figured out."

"How late do you have to work?"

"I have to do the six o'clock news and the ten o'clock. I won't be home 'til after midnight."

Renee's nostrils flared. She loved her husband dearly, especially his smarts and his work ethic. But sometimes James worked *too* hard. He graduated from Texas Lutheran as a media major and hadn't touched the ground since.

He took a job as a cameraman with Channel Six news and worked the trenches for nearly a decade. He had to brave all types of weather and even some dangerous environments in the early days. But eventually James moved up the ladder. He now worked in the studio as a lead videographer.

When she was younger, Renee never dreamed of having a husband as successful as James. But a savings account couldn't keep her warm at night. She rarely complained about his work hours, but today she looked forward to her man being there when she got home.

"My day keeps getting worse," she griped.

"Baby, it's not that bad. You'll still be up when I get home."

"Maybe I will. Maybe I won't."

"I'll make it worth your while," James promised.

Renee smiled. She was certainly eager for him to try. But they had a hurdle in the sex department, and she doubted if James was willing to jump it tonight. *How long has it been?* she wondered. She figured at least three months had passed since the last time she was able to coax him into it. Renee decided she was due, if not because of the time that passed, then at least for the terrible day she'd been having.

"Are you gonna hurt me?" she asked tentatively. Her heart was already starting to race.

After a noticeable pause, James said, "No. But I will make love to you, as a husband should make love to his wife."

That was his typical response. Renee was not deterred.

"What if I don't want you to make love to me?"

"I don't know," he said. "I guess you can go to sleep horny."

Renee found this banter amusing, but she didn't want him to know that.

"I'm having a terrible day," she reiterated. "And it's been a long time since you did that for me."

"It hasn't been that long," James said. "It was Saturday, April 13th."

Renee was stunned by that. "You remember the exact date?"

"When a man does those things to his wife, it's not easy to forget."

"You make it sound like it's hurting you in some way."

"Renee, I'm working just as hard as you are today. I don't want any trouble when I get home."

"You're probably gonna have some."

"I'm not going there with you tonight. I'm serious."

"I understand that you're serious. I want you to be serious."

"Stop playing around."

"Only if you make me."

He sighed loudly into the phone. "I love you, baby. But you're starting to piss me off."

"Perfect," she said. "That's a good start."

"Renee, it's not gonna wor–"

She hung up on him.

≈≈≈≈≈≈≈

The rest of Renee's time at work was surprisingly smooth, but fate would not let her off the hook that easily. When she left the office at 5:30 with Lynda and Michelle, they encountered the worst case of rush-hour traffic Renee had seen all year. Construction on the interstate reduced it to only two lanes. A stalled car in one of those lanes further contributed to the gridlock. Renee drove 18 grueling miles without ever getting her car over ten miles per hour.

She enjoyed her coworkers' company, for the most part, but they ran out of things to talk about after the first twenty minutes. When they finally exited the freeway, it was after 6:30. On a normal day, Renee would've been home and in the shower by then. She raced to drop Lynda off and then Michelle. They were just as tired as she was and didn't comment on her speeding.

When Michelle got out of the car, she said, "Sorry again about the mess back there," reminding Renee that there were still syrup stains in her back seat that were probably caramelized by now after a full day in the Texas heat.

"Don't worry about it," she told her. "I'll take it to the carwash tomorrow. See you on Monday."

Common sense told her to *Go straight home!* at that point, but Renee had to pick up a few things from the store. This weekend she and James didn't have the kids. If Renee could help it, she didn't plan on doing anything at all. She stopped at a Walmart around the corner from Michelle's house, despite the fact that Michelle didn't live in the best neighborhood.

How bad could it be? Renee wondered as she exited her vehicle. She soon got an answer: Very Bad.

Apparently Friday night was the "busy" day for the Walmart in the hood. The customer service line was stretched so long it rounded a corner. It looked to be filled with day-laborers who needed to cash their check and a few scoundrels who wanted to return products they didn't have a bag or receipt for (possibly because they stole the items less than an hour ago).

Stop judging people, Renee told herself as she made her way through aisles that were packed with children, and babies, and employees who were constantly mopping up spills, and women with *more* babies, and the occasional white customer who lived in the neighborhood and was used to seeing all of this but still looked shocked and worried because this is not how the Walmart on the television commercials looks!

By the time Renee made it to the checkout line, she had already decided that she would *never* set foot in that store again – but there was still the matter of getting out of there. She pushed her buggy (which had exactly eight items inside) and fumed because there were ten people ahead of her in the express lane, and two of them had twice as many as the ten item limit! The cashier didn't chastise them at all, which made sense because she was just as bad. She was a teenager, with bleach-blonde highlights and a mouthful of chewing gum that she didn't mind popping loudly as she scanned groceries at her leisure. Renee didn't see how she got anything done with those carefully sculpted fingernails.

Are you fucking kidding me?

But even with all of that, Renee didn't lose it until a woman with an armful of groceries approached and started talking to a woman in line ahead of her. The line-cutter waited until her "friend" took a few steps forward before she squeezed in behind her, thus solidifying her new spot – which just happened to be two spaces ahead of Renee.

"Hey! What do you think you're doing?"

The line-cutter ignored her, but her friend looked back. "What?"

"That lady just cut in line behind you!" Renee said. She didn't want to be the bad guy, but enough was enough. This day had been piling shit on her ever since she got dressed for work nearly twelve hours ago. She couldn't do anything about any of the other stuff, but this time she could.

The line-cutter turned slowly, and Renee realized she picked the wrong woman to confront. The shopper was older than her and taller and twice as big. She didn't wear any makeup, and her hair was already unkempt. Right away Renee knew that this woman would fight her in the middle of the store without a second thought.

"You need to mind your own business," the woman growled.

Renee was so intimidated, she almost said, "Yes, Ma'am," but after an hour and a half drive home (and she still wasn't home!), the last thing she was going to do was let this bully delay her another few minutes.

"No, you need to move to the back of the line," Renee spat. "All of us had to start back there, and so do you."

Renee hoped a few more customers would back her up, but they remained mute.

Losers, she thought. And then she stared in awe as the line-cutter proceeded to curse her out royally. She called Renee all sorts of bitches and hoes, threatened to kick her ass if she didn't mind her own goddamned business and accused Renee of being stuck up – possibly because she was the only woman in the store who didn't wear sneakers with her dress, or a head rag.

The only good thing about the altercation was it was so loud, a security guard came to investigate.

"What's going on here?" He was a big man with a stern disposition. Renee didn't let on how happy she was to see him.

"That lady is cutting in line," she snitched and pointed.

"I was already in line," the bully said. "I just had to go get something right quick, and this bitch started yelling!"

Renee's jaw dropped. She couldn't believe the woman's gall, and she couldn't believe no one was coming to her defense.

"She can't get out of line and come back," Renee said with all of the authority of an official Walmart express lane supervisor. "If you get out, you have to start over at the back." She shot a thumb in that direction. "Plus I've been in line for five minutes, and I never saw her get out."

"You need to mind your damn business," the line-cutter advised.

The security guard made the only logical decision. "Ma'am, you need to get in the back of the line. Everybody wants to get out of here, but you cutting in line and yelling at people ain't helping."

"I didn't cut in line!"

"You just said you got out and came back. If you've been gone for five minutes, you have to start over at the end of the line."

Renee smiled smugly, and the bully surprised everyone by dropping all of the items she was carrying. They fell to the floor loudly, but luckily none of it was glass.

"Forget it, I'll just go home! I ain't got to shop in this goddamned store!"

"That works too, Ma'am. Come on. Right this way."

He gestured towards the exit and was smart enough not to lay a hand on her. The line-cutter shot Renee a rather evil glare before following him out. Renee looked back to the line-cutter's friend and saw that she had the same mean look in her eyes.

"Next in line," the cashier said, and thankfully things got moving again.

≈ ≈ ≈ ≈ ≈ ≈ ≈

53

When she finally made it out of the store, Renee got halfway to her car before she noticed a group of women loitering in the parking lot. She looked back at the store and considered running in that direction, but she saw that the security guard had come outside, too. She was pretty sure nothing would go down with him watching.

But then one of the girls said, "There she go!" and the crowd stepped quickly in Renee's direction. She wasn't surprised to see the line-cutter leading the pack. Renee didn't have time to open her car door before they were close enough for physical contact.

"What's up now?" the largest woman said. "Talk some of that shit you was talking in the store."

Renee couldn't believe this was happening. What had she done to bring on such bad karma? Did she step on a spider this morning?

Still moving towards her car, she said, "I don't want no trouble. I'm going home."

"No, you finna apologize for that shit you pulled in the store," Big Mama said.

Renee saw that her line-cutting accomplice was there to back her up, as were two other girls who looked like they were still in high school.

"All I said was you shouldn't be cutting," Renee offered as she opened her door. She wanted to jump in her car right away, but that would actually put her at a tactical disadvantage, if Big Mama reached inside and grabbed a handful of hair before she got the door closed. Punching *downwards* is always easier than punching up. Plus Renee still had the option of running as long as she was on her feet.

Fear caused goose bumps to sprout on her arms as she considered the possible outcomes. Even if the security guard broke it up, the women could get in an untold number of blows before he got there. Renee had never been in a serious street fight. She gritted her teeth, knowing she had to eat crow a second time that day.

"I'm sorry if I upset you. Now are we done? Come on, you're being silly. There's kids out here. We're better than this."

The bully was over forty, so she had to stop to consider that.

But one of the younger girls said, "Ooh, Mama. She said you *silly!*"

Renee's jaw dropped just as Big Mama balled her fist. Fortunately a male voice interrupted them.

"Is there a problem?"

They all looked back and saw the security guard was headed their way.

Renee took advantage of the brief distraction and jumped in her car. Her door was closed and locked before anyone could react.

"Nope. I'm fine," she yelled through the window as she started her Honda.

She had to beep her horn a couple of times, but the hoodlums eventually parted and allowed her to pass.

CHAPTER THREE
A RUSE WITHIN A RUSE

Renee felt relieved when she left Walmart, but a few miles down the road her anger started to set in. Why did people have to be so stupid? And why was violence such a knee-jerk reaction for some women? It wasn't a black/white thing. It seemed to be a low-income thing. Renee was also upset with herself for being such a wuss. Maybe she should've taken a swing at the big bully. She would've been beaten to a pulp – no doubt about that – but at least she'd have her dignity.

Renee chuckled and shook her head at her own foolishness. The cemetery was filled with people who wanted to *keep it real* and show how tough they were. Renee knew that she made the right move, under the circumstances. But that knowledge didn't make her feel any better.

When her cellphone rang, and she saw her ex-husband's number on the display, Renee quickly decided she wasn't going to take any shit from this particular butt hole. She answered with a mean scowl already in place.

"What do you want, Sherman?"

"Damn, woman. It's like that? No 'Hi' or nothing?"

"Hi," Renee said. "What do you want?"

"Why you mad? You don't even know why I called."

"I'm mad because today has been one of the worst days I've ever had. And don't tell me I don't know what you want. Today's July 5th, which means you're exactly *five days* into the month you're supposed to keep the boys.

"I know you're calling to tell me you can't do it, you got too much shit going on, there's no one there to watch them when you're at work, or some other bullshit reason why you can't maintain your *minimum* responsibility for the two children you helped bring into this world. *That's* what you're calling to tell me."

"Okay. I can see you're upset, so I'll call you tomorrow."

"No, there's no need for you to call me tomorrow," Renee said. "I don't need you to call me until *August 1st*. That's the day you can bring the boys back, Sherman. Until then, we don't have nothing to talk about."

"But I don't have no one to watch them when I go to work," Sherman acknowledged.

"You don't need anyone to watch them. Paul is almost 14. I leave them home alone all the time."

"But I don't want them going through all my stuff," Sherman said. "There's no telling what they'll get into while I'm gone all day."

"That's your problem for not having a good relationship with your sons. You should trust them enough not to go through your stuff."

"You can't trust two little boys in a house by their self."

"Then get a babysitter," Renee suggested.

"I can't afford that. You taking damn near half my check—"

"I'm not taking anything!" she snapped. "You're paying child support to support *your* children. And they're only taking money from your Kroger's check. Don't think I don't know you have another job with Everman ISD. That's probably why you don't want to keep the boys; you're working too damned much."

"I have to work like this to survive," Sherman complained. "You don't know what it's like to see all of those deductions after you worked your fingers to the bone for two weeks. Sometimes I feel like I'm working for nothing."

Renee started to tell him that he didn't know what it was like caring for the boys 90% of the time with barely any input or assistance from their biological father. It was times like this when she truly treasured her husband.

James proposed to her ten years ago and treated the boys like they were his from day one. Truth be told, Renee didn't depend on or really need Sherman's child support. But she was determined that he did provide for his children to some degree. Keeping them every other weekend and for one full month in the summertime was the least he could do.

"Today's Friday," she breathed. "I know you don't work on the weekends, so what's the problem?"

"I know," Sherman said. "I don't have no problem with the weekend. I never complained about keeping them on any of my weekends."

"Yes you have!"

"Okay, but not that much. I'm just saying I can't keep them during the week*days*. I wanted to know if you could take them back on Monday."

Renee really wanted to curse him out. But it wouldn't have done any good. Plus she didn't want her sons to stay anywhere they weren't wanted and appreciated. She knew James wouldn't bat an eye when she told him the kids' month with their father would end in only a week, because Sherman pulled this stunt nine summers in a row.

"Fine. Bring them back on Monday," she said.

"Thanks, Renee. I'm really sorry about this. I'll make it up to you."

She knew that was never going to happen, so she just said, "Goodbye, Sherman."

She called her oldest son Paul on his cellphone when she got off the line with

Sherman. Paul was happy and still excited about spending time with his father. After a few minutes he passed the phone to eleven year old Robert, who was just as thrilled. They didn't know that their father would kick them to the curb again on Monday, and Renee didn't tell them. No sense in ruining the rest of their weekend.

≈≈≈≈≈≈≈

By the time she got home, the sun had already gone away for the day. The house was dark and quiet, but Renee wasn't lonely. She loved having private time to herself. She undressed and slipped into the tub with a glass of Moscato and Fantasia playing on the stereo. Gradually the stress from her hellacious day began to dissipate at the same rate as her bath salts.

James called a few hours later. Renee was in the living room, lounging on the sofa with another glass of Moscato and the television remote in hand. She was in a better mood by then, and she missed her husband. She was excited to hear that he was on his way home.

She told him about the incident at Walmart and about Sherman bringing the boys back on Monday. As expected, James was not upset about her ex-husband's antics.

"That's cool. I wanted to take them fishing in a couple of weeks anyway. I knew he wasn't going to keep them the whole month," he said with a chuckle. "How about you? Are you okay with it?"

"I'm fine. But I did look forward to being alone with you more."

"Me too," James said. "We still have this weekend."

"And tonight," Renee added.

After a pause, James said, "Baby, I told you I'm not doing that tonight."

"But I *need* it," Renee whined.

"No you don't. You're just upset about everything that happened today."

"Even if I had a great day, I would still want it."

"I don't understand you."

"You don't have to. Just give me what I want."

"If you keep pressuring me, I'm going to come home and go straight to sleep. If you be good, I promise to give you a full body massage when I get there."

Renee knew she was probably wrong for rejecting his offer to make love to her, slow and sweet. And she understood why he almost always declined to participate in her fetish. At this moment, they were at opposite ends of the pole. James wanted to make love to his spouse. Renee wanted him to murder her pussy. But regardless of what James said, he would give her what she wanted.

Tonight.

"Alright, I'm not going to ask anymore," she said. "But don't say anything to me when you get home. As a matter of fact, you don't even have to come home. I can take care of myself. I don't need you."

"You can't take care of yourself," James said knowingly. "You don't have what it takes."

He knew it was childish, but James took offense to Renee's use of sex toys. As long as his dick was working properly (which it was), and as long as his wife liked the size (which she did), then Renee didn't need another penis in her life – be it plastic or flesh and blood.

James never denied her in the bedroom, even when she was in one of her twice-a-day modes. She told him she got rid of all of her dildos, but they seemed to keep popping up, usually at times like this.

"Trust me, I can take care of myself," Renee said. "I'm about to bust a nut right now – on your pillow."

"You humping my pillow?"

"Yup. Juices everywhere... And you gonna sleep on it."

James was getting irritated and horny at the same time – which, of course, was exactly what his wife wanted.

"I know what you're doing, and I promise it's not working. When I get home, I'm going to sleep, Renee. I can sleep without a pillow. That's not hurting me."

"Ain't nobody trying to do nothing to you, *James*. You do you, boo. I don't give a *fuuuuuuuck*."

Renee laughed and hung up on him.

≈≈≈≈≈≈≈

It all started three years ago. It was a beautiful day, the third Saturday of March, and the boys were away for the weekend with their father. Renee spent most of the afternoon shopping, and James took offense to her spending habits when she got home. Renee hadn't worked in two years. James thought he'd seen more shopping bags than grocery bags as of late.

He confiscated her credit card, and Renee responded with uncharacteristic pouting. She gave him the cold shoulder and then the silent treatment and then escalated things when she didn't get the response she wanted. She took a shower and entered the den totally nude, carrying a glass of wine. She sat opposite James, who was no longer interested in college hoops. He loved his wife's figure. Every curve. He wanted to taste the beads of water that glistened on her dark brown flesh.

But when he moved to be closer, grinning like a damned fool, Renee shut him down.

"Can't I walk around naked without wanting to have sex? *Damn!*"

She all but snarled at him, and James returned to his seat. He knew she was trying to goad him into an argument, so he pretended not to notice. Renee went to get a second glass of Merlot after she finished the first. She paused near the television to straighten some of the whatnots.

James' dick stretched his shorts, but he returned his attention to the game when she looked his way. After a few minutes, she left the room again. She reappeared and retrieved a duster from one of the shelves. James thought it was pretty low for her to punish him with sex, but he didn't say anything. It was amusing, and he wanted to see how far she'd go with it.

His answer came in the form of a crash that jolted him from his seat. James rushed to the dining room and was surprised to find his still-naked wife "dusting" the fine china that was on display on one of the shelves. As he watched, she poked a second plate with the duster, and it too fell from the perch and shattered on the floor.

"Woman are you crazy?!"

James was never one to get physical with a woman, but his wife standing buck-nekkid in the dining room wantonly breaking dishes was definitely cause for exception. He tried to take the duster, and then he grasped at her arms when Renee refused to give it up. As they struggled, James' immediate concern was to get her precious feet away from the broken glass. He pushed her towards the living room. Renee pushed him back, and a wrestling match ensued.

James' anger began to rise as they struggled, and Renee seemed to be just as incensed. At some point she started pulling and ripping his tee-shirt. James told her that if she wanted some dick, all she had to do was ask. Renee scoffed at the notion and punched him in the chest. One thing led to another, and

James found himself fucking his wife harder and rougher than he ever had. She continued to fight until the sweet end.

When they lay on the floor spent and sweating, with tracks from her weave yanked out and his clothes in tatters on the floor, Renee returned to being her usual lovable self, and James wrestled with the notion that he just tried to *fuck* the crazy out of his wife. Even worse was the fact that it seemed to work.

Renee was hooked on rough sex from that moment on. But James was always hesitant. He loved his wife dearly, and he didn't like the idea of hurting her. Renee insisted that she was never hurt during the whole ordeal, but James didn't see how that was possible. He had pulled hair from her head. Granted it wasn't her hair, but it was sewn in rather tightly.

Renee started to bring home pornographic videos, which James was obliged to watch with her, mostly in wide-eyed fascination. Some of the videos were so wild, James thought the woman was being *raped*, but it was clear the porn stars were willing participants – just like his wife.

James was so baffled, he eventually had to seek counsel from a distant cousin who was also a pastor. Kalvin had never met Renee, and after their conversation, James vowed that they would *never* meet, lest the pastor look at his wife with a kinky awareness.

After telling his side of the story, James asked him, "Is she crazy? This is crazy, right? I know this isn't normal."

Kalvin thought long and hard before he gave his opinion: "I understand how this can be troubling for you. But you are married, James. And she is your wife. And, as you mentioned, she said you're not physically harming her."

"But I've left scratches on her," James protested. "And she's left scratches on me."

"Many couples scratch each other during lovemaking," the pastor replied.

"But she wants to get me *mad*, just so I'll do it," James griped. "I know you're not going to tell me we should be angry with each other during sex."

"Do you believe she's really angry with you?"

James thought back to the naked dining room incident, and he had to shake his head. "No. She just wants to get my attention."

"And are you angry with her, when you make love to her in this way?"

Again James had to shake his head. "She thinks I am, but I'm not. Not really. I just act like I'm mad, so she'll stop acting up."

"Then it sounds like both of you are *acting*," the pastor said. "So this is a form of role playing. This can actually be healthy for a married couple."

James sighed out of exasperation. "But, but sometimes I think I like it too much," he confided. "When I pull her hair, or I'm slapping her, um, her bottom. Like, *hard*. I feel like... I don't know. It's something about it that turns me on, and I don't think it should."

Kalvin's eyes widened for a moment, but again he didn't condemn their acts. "James, if she's turned on by you behaving this way in bed, and you're turned on by the way she's acting and the things she wants you to do, then it's not as bad as you're making it out to be.

"Some couples pretend to be strangers, and they'll meet at a bar for a *one night stand*. It doesn't mean they want a one night stand with others. And I don't think it's wrong for them to be turned on when their spouse pretends to be someone else.

"I do a lot of marriage counseling. From experience I can tell you that when one partner wants something, *less traditional*, done in the bedroom, and the other partner is unwilling to participate, it can lead to frustration, resentment and in the worst cases even affairs and divorce.

"Don't forget, James: A happy wife is a happy life. If it makes your wife happy when you play rough with her, and it excites you as well, I say go for it – as long as nothing truly dangerous is going on."

James left his cousin's church that day still doubtful, but not as much as he was before he talked to him. He wanted to keep his wife happy, and he had to accept that a part of her happiness was dependent on what he considered unusual behavior. He could only do it once every few months, and Renee seemed to accept that.

When that time came, they had a pattern. It was usually sparked by a lot of stress on Renee's part. She'd upset James because she knew he couldn't please her like she wanted under normal circumstances. James in turn upset Renee by refusing to participate. Their anger would be a perfect sexual storm. What Renee didn't know was James was no more upset than she was. They were both pretending.

Renee also didn't know that James had become obsessed with reaching her breaking point.

No!

Stop!

Pleeeeeeeease!

That was like music to his ears.

CHAPTER FOUR
THE FINAL CHAPTER
THE PERFORMANCE

When he walked into his home, James didn't smell anything that even resembled a meal. Not cool. He wasn't one of those *Woman, where's my food?* type of guys, but Renee knew he appreciated dinner after a long day's work. If he got home first, he would do the cooking for her and the boys. But James already knew that he wouldn't be welcomed like a king tonight. Renee would do whatever it took to push him over the edge, be it minor or major.

James proceeded to the kitchen anyway, just to be sure. He deposited his briefcase next to the couch as he passed through the dark living room. The house was completely quiet. The kitchen light was on. James' footsteps were barely audible on the tiles because he was fortunate enough to have a job that allowed him to wear sneakers to work. Not many people making six figures a year could say the same.

The kitchen counters were all bare and clean. The same with the stovetop. James opened the oven, and then he checked inside the refrigerator. When he closed the door, Renee stood in the hallway in all her breathtaking glory. The sight of her made James swallow roughly. His dick immediately began to swell in his boxers.

Renee wore a red robe. That was all. It wasn't closed. James stared at her, his eyes rolling up and down her nude form. He loved his wife's size. She was a little more than a foot shorter than him. Her skin was dark and lovely. She had full lips that were coated with red lipstick. Her natural hair was straight and shoulder-length. Her eyes were relatively small, giving the appearance that her hair was pulled back in a tight ponytail even when it wasn't.

James never thought his wife was overweight. There wasn't an inch of her body that didn't excite him. Her hips and thighs were pleasingly thick. Her breasts were equally swollen. He saw that she shaved her pubic hair, leaving only a small patch.

Renee's feet were bare. Her toenail polish matched her lipstick. James wanted to take her into his arms, but Renee didn't look like she wanted to be taken or even touched, for that matter. She remained mute as she looked him up and down.

James wore a short-sleeved collar shirt with blue jeans. His skin was as dark as hers, which was one of the things she loved about him. The only hair on his head was his thick eyebrows. James weighed more than her, but he was relatively thinner. Where Renee had soft, succulent curves, he had hard sinewy muscles. Next to his work, James' second hobby was his body. He worked out at least three days a week, and the results were mesmerizing. His biceps looked formidable beneath his golf shirt. Even his forearms were sculpted.

James was Renee's lean, mean chocolate dream. The first time she saw him naked, she worried that a fit guy like him might pressure her to slim down as well. But that was never the case. James' love for her physique gave Renee the confidence to love her body as well. She often strutted around naked when the boys were away, which thrilled James to no ends. Renee could tell he was drooling now, but until he mustered the will to punish her, she had to continue punishing him.

She placed a hand on her hip and gave him a sarcastic look. "So, what did you decide?"

James looked into her eyes and said, "About what?"

Renee frowned and rolled her eyes. "Alright. I'll be in there with my boyfriend. You can sleep on the couch tonight. If you want something to eat, it's a frozen pizza in there."

With that, she turned and walked away.

"What'd you say?" James started after her.

Renee increased speed in the hallway. She was surprisingly nimble. James actually tried to catch her, but Renee made it to their bedroom at the end of the hallway before he caught up. She slammed the door closed. By the time James twisted the knob, it was locked from the inside. His nostrils flared as he wiggled the knob. Renee did a lot of foolish things in their sex play, but she never locked him out of his own bedroom.

"What the hell are you doing?" he shouted. "Open this damn door!"

"No!"

He pounded with his fist. "Renee, open this goddamned door! What do you mean you got a boyfriend in there? You talking about a fucking dildo?"

"Don't worry about it!" she shouted. "You didn't want it, so why you tripping?"

"I'm not playing!" James yelled. "Where'd you get it? How long have you had it?"

He wondered how many of her sex toys he'd thrown away in the past few years. Renee never used them for practical reasons; only to piss him off when she couldn't get her way in bed. Most of this sexual fantasy was all for show, but James had a serious problem with

another dick sliding in and out of his wife –
even if it was a plastic wannabe dick. If Renee
wanted to masturbate, she should use her
fingers. If she needed more than that, she'd
have to depend on him.

"Are you gonna open this door, or do I
have to break it down?" James bellowed.

"Break it if you want!" Renee dared him.
"You're the one who'll have to fix it!"

A moment later, James heard the sound
of a pornographic movie playing loudly in the
bedroom. Arguing with her was futile at that
point, because she wouldn't be able to hear him
over the increasingly wild yelps of one of the
porn stars.

James shook his head and took a step
away from the door. He considered kicking it
in, but Renee was right about who'd be
responsible for repairing it. Instead he knelt
and studied the doorknob. He stood with a
smirk and headed back down the hallway. He
continued through the kitchen and unlocked

the door to the garage. Once inside, he found his power drill on a work bench and attached a socket with a screwdriver head.

He returned to his bedroom and quickly disassembled the whole doorknob. He pulled half of it out on his side. The other knob fell to the floor inside the room. Apparently Renee was too caught up in her debauchery to notice. When James pushed the door open, he was surprised (but not too surprised) to see his wife sprawled out on the bed totally nude. Her eyes were glued to the flat screen television mounted above their biggest dresser. James saw that she did indeed have a boyfriend with her, and the lucky bastard was fully submerged in her sweet, pink folds. The dildo was all black, and it had more length than girth.

As James watched, she worked the toy in and out slowly. Her hips were already starting to squirm on the mattress. Her mouth hung open. Her bare flesh made James rock hard in seconds. He followed her gaze to the television and saw a Brazilian woman being abused by three cock strong men. When his eyes returned to his wife, James saw that she was looking at him. She didn't have the decency to stop or slow her masturbation, which ticked James off even more.

"You gon' lock me out of my own bedroom so you can do this shit?" he barked.

"Shut up," she said. "I'm almost done."

James was shocked to see her increase the speed of her strokes.

He didn't rush in right away because as much as he despised her toys, the scene before him was sexy as hell. Renee began to hump the fake dick, harder and harder, until her ass left the mattress each time. The look on her husband's face made her heart thunder. Her clitoris shuddered in anticipation of the punishment she was sure to receive for this stunt.

James subconsciously wiped his mouth with the back of his hand. He slowly pulled his shirt over his head. When he met Renee's eyes again, she had a sneer on her face.

"I don't know why you doing that. Don't come over here. I'm – *ooh* – I'm good!"

When he got his shirt off, Renee nibbled her lip as she marveled at his perfection. Even with no body oil, the definition of his muscles was awe-inspiring. Renee was already close to an orgasm. The sight of her man's half naked body as he watched her masturbate nearly pushed her over the edge – especially the dark, angry look in his eyes. James began to march in her direction, and Renee's blood raced even hotter.

"Give it here!"

"No!"

Renee removed the dildo as she scooted away from him on the mattress. When she looked up again, James hovered over her, reaching with both hands but unable to secure the sex toy.

"Stop fighting me!"

He grabbed her shoulders and rolled her onto her back. Renee screamed as he mounted her, with a knee on either side of her torso. She held the dildo tightly; hugged to her chest, while she warded off his attempts with her free hand. James looked like he might pummel her. Renee's heart rattled in the back of her throat. She felt her whole pussy spasm. It was wonderful!

"Stop! Get off!"

She tried to buck him, but her husband's superior position was secure. And he was strong! He restrained her free arm with one hand and wrestled for the dildo with the other. Renee was super wet. James' hand brushed her nipples, which caused them to harden and stand erect. He wanted to bite one of them until she cried out in pain – or pleasure. Either way.

"You gon' make me–"

"Here! Take it!"

She meant to throw the sex toy over his shoulder, so she'd have time to plan her next move while he went to retrieve it. But James reached up and caught it in midair. Unfortunately he grabbed it at the base, and the head flopped back into his face, smacking him in the corner of the mouth.

All movement stopped. That was truly accidental, and Renee couldn't hide her shock. Her eyes widened at the same rate as James'. He let go of her and touched the side of his mouth gingerly. He looked down at her with a perplexed expression, and then he slowly climbed off of her and headed for the adjacent restroom. Renee's body went numb. She was afraid and apologetic and unsure of herself, but at the same time she was incredibly horny. It was crazy awkward!

The Brazilian girl continued to suck and fuck merrily on the television screen as Renee got up to follow her husband. She found James leaning over the sink; inspecting his mouth in the bathroom mirror. Renee's heart knocked hard in her chest as she stood behind him.

James' back fanned out like an angry cobra. Even the muscles straddling his spine were well-defined. Renee stood on her toes, trying to peer over his shoulder. She and James locked eyes in the mirror. His were dark and ominous. His bushy eyebrows bunched together. Renee emitted a startled gasp when she saw that his bottom lip was starting to swell.

Before she could muster an apology, James turned quickly and grabbed her roughly by the shoulder. He yanked her into the bathroom, and moved his grip to the back of her neck. Renee screamed (this one was totally real) as he forced her face towards the mirror.

"You see this shit?" James growled.

They were both close to the mirror now, and there was no doubt about the bruise.

"I got to go to work with this shit on my face! You see what your fucking games did?"

Renee's heart was thundering. Her eyes were as big as quarters. Regardless of how rough they played in the past, there was always a small part of her that knew that James loved her, and he would never cause her any arm. Now she wasn't so sure.

But even with this uncertainty, she still wanted him to take is aggression out on her body. She wanted him to grab her hair and drag her to the bedroom and use his dick as a weapon until she cried for mercy.

"I'm sorry," she breathed.

"You sorry?"

He let go of her neck. Renee barely had time to brace herself before he slapped her ass with an open palm. The **SMACK!** sounded off in the small room like a cymbal. It hurt like hell! Renee's butt cheek was instantly on fire, and at the same time she felt a pleasant shudder between her legs. She couldn't stop another frightened scream from escaping her.

Her fight or flight instincts kicked in, and she chose to get the hell out of there. But James grabbed her with both hands before she had time to flee. He spun her quickly and took a brief moment to kick the lid down on the toilet before he planted her ass there. Renee tried to get to her feet, but he grabbed a handful of hair on the side of her head and held firm.

"Aaaah!"

"So you wanna hit me in the face with your *boyfriend*?" James growled as he fished the toy from the sink. "What else you do with this?" He waved the toy in her face.

Renee opened her mouth to respond, and she was shocked to find it suddenly filled with her slick, plastic phallus. It was wet with her essence. The taste was scandalous and exotic. James pushed the dildo deeper into her mouth and kept a grip on her head with his other hand. Renee's eyes bugged. She was appalled! She screamed through her nose, and James grinned wickedly.

"This is your boyfriend, right? What's wrong? You don't like him now? He can't get no action?"

Renee grabbed his hand and tried to push it away. James shoved her head back until the toilet's cool tank dug into her upper back. This was erotic as hell, but James had never taken it to this level. Surprisingly, Renee found that she was turned on even more. James' anger was a fierce intoxicant that set her soul and pussy on fire. Saliva started to spill from her mouth as he worked the dick in and out.

Unwilling to show him how much she was starting to enjoy this, Renee clamped down with all thirty-two choppers and growled. She shook her head fiercely, like a wolf with a freshly caught bunny. James didn't expect that at all. He tried to remove the toy as Renee continued gnawing on it. When he finally got it free, the dildo was a mangled facsimile of its former self. James couldn't believe she resorted to such savagery.

Still gripping her hair, he swallowed hard and asked, "Is that how you treat your boyfriend?"

"Anything you put in my mouth is getting ate the fuck up," Renee promised. Her teeth were still bared. She had spit on her lips and dribbling down her chin. James was both terrified and eager.

"Is that right?" He dropped the dildo and ripped his pants open with his free hand.

"Don't do it," Renee warned.

James ignored her. He pulled his pants and boxers down past his butt, and his dick sprang up hard and proud. Rene's heart swelled at the sight of it. It was thick and venous with plenty of length, too. He thrust his hips forward and pulled Renee's face to him at the same moment. He grabbed the other side of her head when his meat encountered two rows of unyielding teeth.

"Open your mouth," he demanded.

"No—"

That was all the opening he needed. James forced his dick inside her mouth and was greeted with a warm wetness that almost made him shoot his load within seconds. Rather than wait for her to respond, he began to make love to her face. Renee screamed and mumbled all sorts of insults through her nose, but she did not follow through with her promise to bite it off. Instead James felt her tongue massaging him expertly. Her cheeks went concave as she began to suck him further down her throat.

"*Goddamn*," James breathed. He was sweating, and Renee was sweating, and all of the adrenaline was more than he could keep a lid on. "I'ma cum," he threatened.

Renee's mouth watered even more at the thought of his essence coating her tongue. She loved being restrained while he explored her cavities at will, but she still had a role to play.

Without warning, she shoved him hard in the stomach with both hands. James was caught off guard, and he went flying into the wall behind him. Before he could straighten himself, Renee darted past him and was on the run again.

She got a nice head start because James' pants were wrapped around his ankles, and his shoes were still on. He stomped and kicked like a madman to free himself of the clothing. He caught up with his wife in the living room and tackled her on the sofa. They were both completely nude now. It was hard to tell where his skin ended and hers started in the darkness.

They wrestled briefly before James got the upper hand. He forcibly bent her over the arm of the couch. With her fat ass in his face, his dick jumped, and pre-cum filled the shaft. He smacked her hard on the same cheek as before and shoved his meat in her wet pussy when she screamed. He plunged deep and hard, all the way to the hilt on the first stroke and immediately started pounding away with his wife's screams in one ear and the porn star's screams still audible from the bedroom.

SPLACK!
SPLACK!
SPLACK!

Damn, she was so wet! And tight! Renee's slippery walls gripped his dick like a fist, and he knew she was already cumming.

"Uh! Ahh! *James!*"

Renee's whole body was blazing – especially her bruised ass cheek – but her pussy was molten lava. James' dick punched the back end with every stroke, and the bottom of his shaft provided constant titillation to her clitoris.

"*Damn!*" she bellowed. "Oh shit! Goddamn!"

Her pussy opened even more with her release, and James was eager to claim every bit of new real-estate. He slapped her ass again, and then gripped both of her butt cheeks like he was holding on for dear life. Renee's hips were wider than his. James pumped like he was trying to squeeze his whole body between her cheeks.

Renee's orgasm was a huge ball of energy that originated between her legs and sent tendrils of pleasure and pain in every direction, like the fire radiating off the sun. Her clitoris was a hard, throbbing knob which fed off the friction James' dick continued to supply.

"*Oh! Oh, James!*"

Renee's heart fluttered. There was a dull, white explosion in her chest and behind her eyes. She felt her climax in every single part of her body – even her hair. For the next twenty seconds, she could feel the pressure from the sustained ass-pounding her husband was delivering, but she couldn't hear the sound of James' thighs smacking her own because of the blood rushing past her ears.

"Okay," she breathed. *"Please. Please..."*

She reached back to push him away. James was having none of that.

"You want me to stop? You trying to stop me?"

Renee tried to speak but couldn't. Her eyes swam in their sockets, and the room started to spin as well. James backed away suddenly. Renee was frozen in place and time with her face in the couch cushions, and her wet, bruised ass still propped up on the arm of the sofa. James stared at her wide open, leaking pussy for a moment before he walked around the couch and hoisted her into the air.

Renee lost all sense of equilibrium until James deposited her on the sofa again. Now her back was where her face had just been. Her legs dangled over the front of the couch. James moved the coffee table out of the way before he dropped to his knees and settled between her thick thighs. Without so much of a *How you doing?* he invaded her again – all the way on the first stroke – and commenced to jabbing her wet opening like Ali in his prime.

"Uhn! *Baby, wait!*"

Renee's eyes flashed open, and she stared at the sexy, black beast having his way with her. She knew James was punishing her for the dildo to the face. It was thrilling and fantastic. She fought hard to keep a smile off her face as her pussy got even juicier for him. James' dick was electrifying. He re-charged her clitoris, and it began to throb anew.

James hoisted her legs in the air suddenly and propped them in the crook of his arms. He knees left the floor, and his toes dug into the plush carpet until he was damned near standing up in her pussy. His dick was still rock hard. He had enough leverage to pump his hips feverishly, and now it hurt! The pain was excellent! So divine.

"Nuh! Uh! No!"

She pushed against his chest. James ignored her pleas. He continued to pound her box like this might be the last pussy he ever got. Sweat was starting to roll down his face. His chest and stomach muscles glistened with perspiration. The sofa springs gave a little beneath them with each thrust, but not enough. Renee caught the full brunt of the impact, and she was delighted to feel another orgasm bubbling around her clitoris. Her sweet, pink walls squeezed James' dick like contractions, and she knew that he felt it, too.

He paused long enough to ask, "You want me to stop?"

Renee wanted no such thing, but she knew that she was insatiable. Her body could never keep up with her desires. But regardless of how much she could physically take, the thought of not getting her second orgasm was unfathomable. From the way her coochie was throbbing, she could tell it was going to be just as, if not more powerful than the first one.

"No. Don't – don't stop."

James hoisted her into the air again and deposited Renee with her chest on the sitting portion of the couch. Her face was now against the back cushions. James dropped to his knees a second time. He spread her legs and wrapped them around his waist wheelbarrow style before plunging balls deep again.

"Aaaah!"

Renee's scream was muffled because her face was crammed into the sofa, but not for long. James grabbed a fistful of her hair and pulled her head up until Renee felt like he had her hogtied. All the while he continued to beat her pussy mercilessly.

Renee felt totally dominated. There was no fight left in her. This was the moment she relished the most. She thought she might cry tears of pure bliss. She felt a huge shudder that made everything below her belly button convulse and tingle. Her orgasm felt like it was taking everything from her, even her breaths. This was the best ever. James continued to pound harder and harder.

SPLACK!
SPLACK!
SPLACK!
"Aaah! Baby! Damn!"
James followed her scream with a huge moan of his own, because rather loosen up after this unprecedented abuse, his wife's nookie squeezed him tighter and tighter. He knew he couldn't last much longer, but he was

determined not to blow until she told him to stop. That was a necessity.

He felt her body trembling. He heard her gasping for air. The muscles in her powerful legs flexed as if in the throes of a seizure, but he wouldn't release his grip on her thighs. He looked down and saw Renee's cum creaming at the base of his dick.

Oh, damn.

He had to look away. But then he looked down again. It was a filthily beautiful sight. James was so captivated by the juices coating his dick, he almost didn't notice that his wife had given the word.

"Okay, baby!" she squealed. *"Baby, please! Pleeeeease!"*

James let her hair and legs go and allowed her knees to slide to the floor. Renee fell forward and began to suck precious air as her walls continued to convulse and massage her husband. Her pussy was nearly numb, but she felt James stroking. Slower now. Easy. He fully submerged with each thrust but was not pushing hard enough to cause her any pain.

After a dozen smooth pumps he told her, "I'm cumming, baby."

Renee couldn't respond, but her heart leapt up her throat when she felt his dick grow even harder as it pulsed and pumped his man juices inside her. She moaned softly, loving the passion he continued to bestow upon her. She was completely satisfied. She had the best husband in the world.

"Baby, I love you," he whispered. "This is the best."

His body shuddered, and an exhausted smile parted Renee's lips. James loved sweet and sensual lovemaking. And no matter how things started, he always got what he wanted.

In the end.

THE END
BY KEITH THOMAS WALKER

ABOUT THE AUTHOR

Keith Thomas Walker, known as the Master of Romantic Suspense and Urban Fiction, is the author of more than a dozen novels, including *Fixin' Tyrone*, *Dripping Chocolate* and *The Realest Ever*. Keith enjoys reading, poetry and music of all genres. Originally from Fort Worth, Keith is a graduate of Texas Wesleyan University.

Visit him at www.keithwalkerbooks.com.